The FEEL GOOD Book

TODD PARR

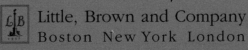

Megan Tingley Books
Little, Brown and Company
Boston New York London

☆ This book is
dedicated to everyone.
FEEL GOOD! ☆

Especially to all those who have made me feel good:
Bully, Tammy, Jerry, Dad, Candy, Grandma, Liz, Gerry,
Dawn, Sandy, Sara, Bill, Karen, Greg, and Jane.

I love you,
Todd

ALSO BY TODD PARR:

The Best Friends Book
Big & Little
Black & White
The Daddy Book
Do's and Don'ts
The Feelings Book
Funny Faces
Going Places
It's Okay to Be Different
The Mommy Book
My Really Cool Baby Book
The Okay Book
Things That Make You Feel Good/
Things That Make You Feel Bad
This Is My Hair
Underwear Do's and Don'ts
Zoo Do's and Don'ts

First Edition

Library of Congress Cataloging-in-Publication Data
Parr, Todd.
  The feel good book / Todd Parr. — 1st ed.
    p. cm.
  "Megan Tingley Books."
  Summary: Relates things that make people feel good.
  ISBN 0-316-07206-0
    [1. Happiness — Fiction.] I. Title
PZ7.P2447 Fdg 2002
[E] — dc21   2001050478

10 9 8 7 6 5 4 3 2 1

NIL

Printed in Italy

Giving a great, big hug feels good

Eating carrots with a bunny feels good

Getting tickled feels good

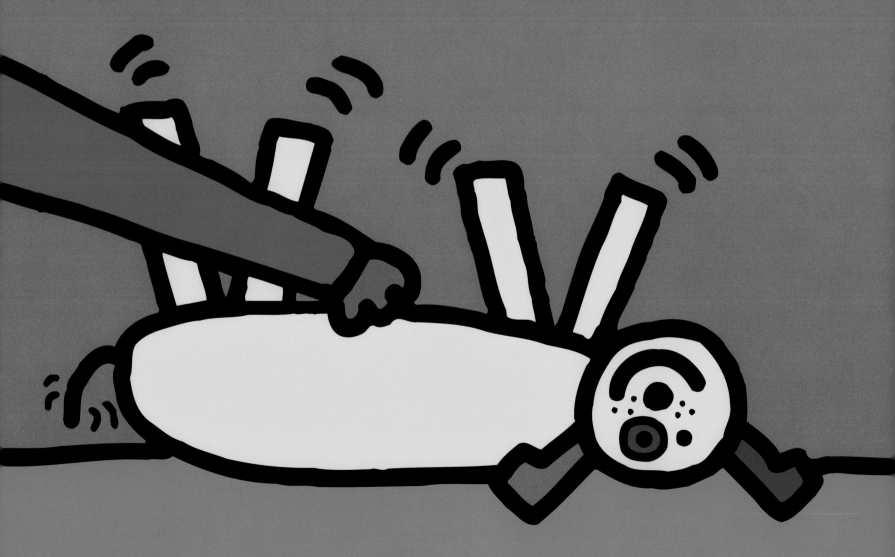

Showing the new kid around feels good

Rubbing noses feels good

Visiting a sick friend feels good

Crying when you're sad feels good

Catching snowflakes on your tongue feels good

Reading a book under a tree feels good

Having a ladybug land on your hand feels good

Sharing your treats feels good

Waiting for the tooth fairy feels good

Saying "I love you" in sign language feels good

Playing under the sprinkler feels good

Making a new friend feels good

Making sounds like a monkey feels good

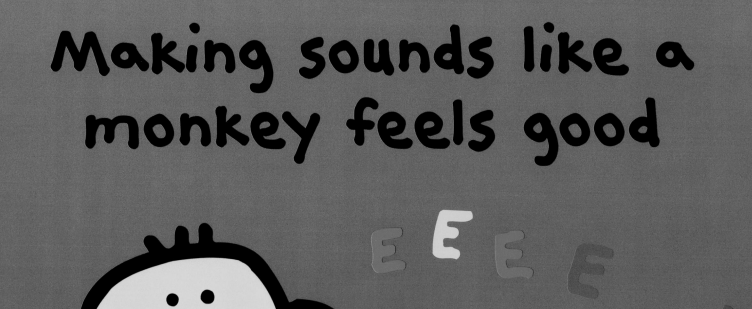

Seeing fireflies outside your window feels good

Letting a kitten lick your fingers feels good

Brushing your teeth with
strawberry toothpaste
feels good

Learning how to count to 8 with a spider feels good

Being brave feels good

Taking a nap with a giant stuffed animal feels good

Being together feels good

It FEELS GOOD to think about all the things that make you FEEL GOOD.

Rubbing my dog's tummy makes me FEEL GOOD— and him, too. What things make you FEEL GOOD?

LOVE,
Todd